A NORTH-SOUTH PAPERBACK

Critical praise for
The Return of Rinaldo, the Sly Fox

"This sequel . . . will delight young readers. . . . Clever and filled with Scieszka-like wit, *Return* . . . is complemented by illustrations that flavor the text with just the right touch of whimsy. One can only hope that this fox will make yet another comeback before too long." *School Library Journal*

"There's enough humor to motivate many readers, especially those who took to the original *Rinaldo, the Sly Fox.*" *Booklist*

"Good light reading." *Kirkus*

The Return of
Rinaldo,
the Sly Fox

by Ursel Scheffler

PICTURES BY
Iskender Gider

TRANSLATED BY
J. Alison James

North-South Books
NEW YORK

Copyright © 1993 by Nord-Süd Verlag AG, Gossau Zürich, Switzerland
First published in Switzerland under the title *Der schlaue Fuchs Rinaldo plant neue Tricks*
English translation copyright © 1993 by North-South Books Inc.

First published in the United States, Great Britain, Canada,
Australia, and New Zealand in 1993 by North-South Books,
an imprint of Nord-Süd Verlag AG, Gossau Zürich, Switzerland.
First paperback edition published in 1995.

Distributed in the United States by North-South Books Inc., New York.

Library of Congress Cataloging-in-Publication Data
Scheffler, Ursel
[Schlaue Fuchs Rinaldo plane neue Tricks. English]
The return of Rinaldo, the sly fox / by Ursel Scheffler : pictures
by Iskender Gider : translated by J. Alison James.
Summary: Rinaldo the sly fox is up to his old tricks, eluding Bruno
the duck detective and acquiring riches through his trickery
until he is outfoxed by a clever cat.
[1. Foxes—Fiction. 2. Animals—Fiction] I. Gider, Iskender, ill. II. Title.
PZ7. S3425Re 1993 [E]—dc20 93-17677
ISBN 1-55858-227-4 (TRADE BINDING)
1 3 5 7 9 TB 10 8 6 4 2
ISBN 1-55858-228-2 (LIBRARY BINDING)
3 5 7 9 LB 10 8 6 4 2
ISBN 1-55858-412-9 (PAPERBACK)
1 3 5 7 9 PB 10 8 6 4 2

A CIP catalogue record for this book
is available from The British Library.

Printed in Belgium

Contents

Rinaldo Slips His Knots

A Hare ran through the woods. He was hopping happy. The sun shone. The hunters were on holiday. His pack was full of fresh carrots. The only thing missing was a shady picnic spot. He was getting hungry. Then he saw a bench at the edge of the woods. Perfect. Whistling cheerfully, the Hare sat down and chomped on a carrot.

What was that? He heard something in
the bushes. It sounded like someone
moaning. He turned around and called,
"Who's there?"

"Helf! Helf!" came a muffled voice.

The Hare pushed aside the branches.
There was a bundle of knots. Knots and fur.
A talking furball!

"Helf, flease helf me!" said the furball.

"Who are you?" asked the Hare.

"I ah Winalbo, de eshape arbist," said the
hoarse voice. "My wast twick wend wong!
Please undie me!"

The friendly Hare didn't wait another
moment. He got out his pocketknife and cut
the ropes. Out came a rather rumpled Fox.

Rinaldo shook his matted fur. He seemed
to grow bigger and bigger. The Hare was
frightened.

"Don't worry!" said the Fox. "I am
the famous circus artist Rinaldo the Great.
I was just trying out a new trick: the
double-trouble slipknot."

"I see," said the Hare.

"You saved my life," said Rinaldo. "I am in
your debt. For now, though, I must be off.
My fans are waiting. Thanks a million!"

The Fox had only just disappeared when
there came another rustling in the bushes.

"Get your paws up or I'll shoot!" bawled
an angry voice.

"Oh dear . . . oh my . . ." stuttered the
Hare. "Are you a robber?" He was looking
down the big black barrel of a peashooter.

"Of course not, carrot-brain! I'm Bruno,
the Duck Detective. We are picking up a
dangerous criminal. Where is he hiding? I
left him tied up right there on the ground."
Bruno stared at the spot.

"Did you let him go?" he thundered.

The Hare shook with fear.

Bruno fingered the pieces of rope. "Sliced clean through," he growled. "Empty your pockets, Mr. Hare."

The Hare handed him his carrot and pulled out his pocketknife.

"Aha!" shouted Bruno. "Here we have it. The evidence!" He took the Hare by the arm. "You are under arrest, Mr. Hare. For aiding and abetting a criminal."

So the poor Hare left his perfect picnic spot and was taken to the Feathertown jail. But not Rinaldo.

Rinaldo Spends a Night in Jail

Rinaldo leaped and capered for joy. Hiding a safe distance away, he saw the poor Hare taken off in the police car that was intended for him.

"That was a lucky break," thought Rinaldo. "But what should I do now? Bruno will be searching high and low for me."

Then he thought of a plan. The last place Bruno would look was in his very own town. Rinaldo ran off.

When he got to Feathertown, Rinaldo picked up a few provisions. He borrowed some eggs from the Weasel's henhouse. Then he snatched some vegetables from Bruno's own garden.

As he slipped through the dark streets, he came upon the jail.

There was the poor Hare, looking out of the window. Rinaldo thought he should at least give the Hare one of Bruno's carrots, but then he had a better idea.

Rinaldo quickly borrowed a large file and got to work. Soon he had sawed through the bars of the jail cell.

"There is still some justice in the world," said the Hare thankfully. He kicked up his heels and hopped away, across the moonlit cabbage field.

Rinaldo grinned. He knew that the Hare's escape would drive Bruno crazy.

Rinaldo was getting tired. He wanted to sleep, but where would he be safe? Rinaldo chuckled. "I'll just stay here. This is the one place he would never look for me!"

The next morning Rinaldo climbed out of the cell. "I just wish I could stay to see Bruno's face when he finds the empty cell!"

Rinaldo Finds
the Road to Riches

When Feathertown was out of sight,
Rinaldo built himself a fire and roasted a
potato for breakfast. Full of food and full of
tricks, he went on his way. Soon he came
upon a garage.

Rinaldo had always wanted to own a
garage. Filling up cars and taking the money
appealed to him. This particular garage
belonged to a couple of Raccoons.

"How's business?" asked Rinaldo. He was already scheming.

"Bad," complained Mr. Raccoon. "It's been bad ever since they put in that new road from Pawsburg to Tailtown. Now the traffic misses us completely."

"Maybe I could help you," suggested Rinaldo. "I am Rinaldo Moneytaker—sorry, Moneymaker. I specialize in helping businesses in trouble."

"How could you help us?" asked Mr. Raccoon. "I think we're beyond help."

"Trust me," said Rinaldo, looking innocent and eager. "I'll put the jump back in your pump!"

Casually he put his hands in his pockets and wandered around the garage. "Not bad," he commented. "Lovely location."

Rinaldo spun on his heel. "Wait! I think . . . Yes, I have it! I've got a plan. But first let's write up a contract."

"My wife has a good deal of experience in writing up contracts," said Mr. Raccoon.

"Good. Let's keep things simple: I'll bring in the customers, you give me half the money."

"Agreed," said Mrs. Raccoon.

"You'll need to wash all the cars that come here to fill up," the Fox added.

"My husband loves washing cars," said Mrs. Raccoon.

"I'm a natural," said Mr. Raccoon.

Rinaldo put a big sign out on the highway.

Fill Up at **Foxy Motors**.
The Greatest Treasures Lie off the Beaten Track
Free Car Wash Included!

When people saw the sign saying "Free Car Wash," they happily went out of their way to the garage. Soon Mr. Raccoon filled up his days washing cars. Mrs. Raccoon filled up car after car. And sly old Rinaldo filled up his pockets with money.

Then Rinaldo found out that another big road nearby was in rough shape.

So he put up a second sign:

Caution: Road closed ahead
Detour on Old Bear Highway

So cars started coming to Foxy Motors from all directions.

Rinaldo rubbed his hands.

The funny thing was, every time the potholes were fixed, new ones appeared.

That was a riddle only the Fox could explain.

Rinaldo Has a Brainstorm

Business got better and better at Foxy Motors. And because the Raccoons could do all the work themselves, the Fox sat lazily in the sun and listened to the lovely ring of the cash register.

One afternoon Rinaldo had another idea. Why just fill up your car—why not fill up your head as well?

He put up another sign:

Announcing a sensation:
The new Think Tank
Increase your brain power in 10 minutes
Reduced rates due to popular demand

The first one to come along was a Stag driving a fancy sports car. He looked at the sign, grinned, and said, "Thank you, but my head is heavy enough already!" He laughed at his own joke.

When the Stag paid his bill, the Fox gave him the wrong change, but the Stag didn't notice.

The Fox shook his head and said, "Didn't count his change! His brain must have grown right out of his head with his antlers."

Soon others came. But no one was interested.

Think Tank This Way

"You can't fool me,"
squawked the Crow.

"I don't have time,"
said the Deer.

"I'm already very wise,"
hooted the Owl.

"My head is too hard,"
blurted the Antelope.

"Do you have a permit?"
snarled the Cat.

"Don't try to trick me!"
quacked the Duck.

"I will not be
defeated!" said
Rinaldo. "I'll
find someone
to fall for this."

Then along came a little Pig pulling a wagon filled with delicious-looking groceries. He was out of breath from climbing the hill.

"A Think Tank—what is that?" he asked.

"It is something that makes you more intelligent," said the Fox.

"That's great!" said the Pig. "My motto is you can never have enough. See all this food? You never know when you're going to get hungry. Certainly I could use some more brains. Who couldn't?"

"Have a seat," said the Fox. "You're in luck. The miraculous machine is ready to enlighten you. As a first-time customer you are entitled to a special rate."

"What a bargain," said the Pig. "Why, it's almost too good to be true."

The Pig sat down on the rusty garden bench. Rinaldo settled earphones on his head. A cheerful medley of tunes poured out. Then Rinaldo stuck a pair of mirrored sunglasses on the Pig's snout.

"Relax, just relax," murmured the Fox. "Wisdom is moments away."

The Pig closed his eyes. The words were
so soothing and the music so soft, and he
was so tired from pulling the heavy cart, that
soon he fell sound asleep.

Rinaldo quickly unpacked the Pig's
groceries and whipped up a delicious lunch
for all his friends.

When the Pig awoke, he was furious.

"You robbed me!" he shouted. "You put me to sleep and then ate all my food!"

"You're a fine one to speak. You still owe me money," the Fox reminded him.

"I owe *you* money!" squealed the Pig. "What for?"

"For using the Think Tank."

"You swindler! You thief!" cried the Pig. "No one can become more intelligent using a pair of sunglasses and a rusty bench!"

"I disagree," said the Fox firmly. "Now you're intelligent enough not to trust a sly Fox. It is obvious that the Think Tank has worked perfectly."

The poor Pig didn't know what to say.

Everyone laughed about how Rinaldo had tricked the Pig. They told the story to all their friends. Pretty soon word got around town, and it wasn't long before it came to the ears of Bruno the Duck Detective.

He pulled up to Foxy Motors in his spinach-green police car and questioned Mr. Raccoon.

"Does a rotten scoundrel named Rinaldo live here?" he asked.

"Aren't you rude!" said Mr. Raccoon. "What would you want with him, anyway?"

Rinaldo overheard the conversation. He didn't hesitate an instant: he scooped all the money from the cash register into his pockets and disappeared out the back door.

Rinaldo Turns Rocks into Riches

The Fox trudged along until he came to Stonytown. There he met a Mole sitting on the edge of his field. The Mole was desperate. His crops were miserable!

"If only I could get rid of this land," he whimpered.

"Sell it," suggested the Fox.

"To whom?" said the Mole. "It's full of rocks. Now I know why they call this Stonytown!"

"Sell it to me," said the Fox. "I like the view."

He got the land dirt cheap.

But Rinaldo didn't spend money just for a view. He had a plan. He was going to turn those stones into gold.

Rinaldo wandered into Stonytown to have lunch.

"I would like to build myself a country house on land I just bought from the Mole," he said to the Hen who ran The Golden Goose. "Do you know someone who could dig me a well?"

"Yes," said the Hen. "My friend the Rooster is a great dowser. He can help you."

The
Golden
Goose

A few days later Rinaldo showed the
Rooster his field.

"It'll be difficult," said the Rooster as he
took up his dowsing stick. "But this piece of
wood has found many an underground
spring." The Rooster walked over the land
with the stick pointed toward the ground.

At one spot the stick wiggled vigorously.

"Here it is! This is where you'll find water," he said, and he set down a stone to mark the place.

The Fox paid the Rooster and smiled to himself as he watched him leave.

After a few days Rinaldo phoned the Rooster.

"I've been digging and digging in that spot, but I haven't found any water. I want my money back."

"Impossible. My dowsing stick never fails. You must not have dug deep enough," the Rooster argued. "Tell you what. I'll bring along a well borer and dig it myself."

The next day the Rooster arrived with his borer.

"That will certainly do a better job than my spade," said Rinaldo.

"Learn something new," said the Rooster, and he rammed the borer into the ground. It dug quickly through the loose earth. Then the Rooster got a surprise. Oil spurted out from the hole instead of water!

"Oil!" complained the Fox. "What can I do with oil? I need water."

"Psst!" whispered the Rooster. His eyes were glistening with greed. "This is terrible. You could be thrown in jail for damaging the environment because you have spilled oil on the land!"

"I don't want to go to jail!" whined the Fox. "Oh, this land is ruined. If only I could get rid of it. Then I wouldn't have to worry about the oil."

"Well," said the crafty Rooster. "Seeing as how my dowsing got you into this mess, I feel it is my duty to buy the land from you. I'd be able to pay you well for it."

"All right then," said the craftier Fox. "It's a deal."

So Rinaldo sold the land to the oil-greedy Rooster for a ton of money.

It was hard for the Fox not to show his delight. Stonytown had become a gold mine, and the field of rocks had made him a fortune!

And the Rooster? He got a nasty surprise when he found out that the oil well was just a buried oil drum!

Rinaldo Meets
His Match

Now Rinaldo was filthy rich! He bought himself a speedy sports car, stayed in the most expensive hotels, and treated himself to luxuries. He even bought a suitcase with three safety locks, where he kept all his cash.

"La-di-da. I think I'll take a trip to Glittertown!" he said to himself one morning. It had always been his dream to see the ocean.

On the way
the Fox sang
a little song:

> There is a Fox who's very clever.
> He's the greatest Fox who ever
> Roamed the country acting slick,
> Ready with a scheme or trick.
> The Duck may chase him to and fro,
> But he is always on the go.
> He's always ready, lying in wait—
> Hurray, hurray for Rinaldo the Great!

He was the coolest, most cunning Fox in the world. Just think of the things he could do!

Then he spotted her: a beautiful Cat. Rinaldo was dazzled.

He slammed on the brakes.

The Cat had emerald-green eyes and silky fur. Rinaldo had never seen such a beautiful Cat in his life.

"What's your name?" she asked as she looked the Fox up and down.

"I am Rinaldo Richman," he answered, and he winked at her. "I'm driving to Glittertown. On business."

"Oh really? I'm going there too. I have just been given the leading role in a new film." She spoke casually. "Unfortunately, last I heard they still hadn't cast the leading man."

"Is that so?" asked the Fox eagerly. He lifted his chin and looked slyly at himself in the mirror.

"You're not interested in acting, are you?" asked the Cat. "You have the perfect look."

"Me? You mean me? Well, I don't know . . ."

"I could phone my agent in Glittertown and ask him if the part is still available," said the Cat.

"Why don't I stop at the next luxury hotel and order us some lunch," said the Fox generously. "You could phone from there."

Soon the Fox spotted the perfect hotel, overlooking the beach. The Fox parked his car. "You know," he said lightly, showing her his suitcase, "I have an entire fortune in here."

A short while later the Fox and the Cat
sat on the terrace of the hotel, eating lunch.
The Fox had three servings of tortellini
because it was so delicious.

"While we're waiting for our dessert, I'll
just phone my agent," said the Cat.

"Of course," said the Fox. He tried not to
show how excited he was about becoming a
movie star.

"Could I just borrow your keys for a
moment?" She smiled sweetly. "I left my
address book in your car."

"Of course, my dear," said Rinaldo.

After a while the waiter brought a note:

My Dear Rinaldo:
Cat got your tongue? She's got your car
and your money! Ciao! Meow!

Rinaldo was speechless.

That thieving feline! If he ever ran across her again, he would clip her claws.

Rinaldo was penniless with a bill to pay.
But that had never stopped him before.
Especially if he'd just eaten a delicious meal.
Besides, he needed to do a little something
to get Bruno's attention.

Rinaldo jotted down a name and address
on the back of the bill. "Just put this on my
account, please," he said to the waiter. "I'm
Bruno, the famous detective, you know."

And with that, he took off for the woods.

Millennium Elementary School
17830 South 84th Avenue
Tinley Park, Illinois 60477
(708) 532 - 3150

About the Author

Ursel Scheffler was born in Nuremberg,
a German city where many toys are made. She
has written over one hundred children's books,
which have been published in fifteen different
languages. She has a special liking for foxes and
other two- and four-legged tricksters—as you
can see from this story.

About the Illustrator

Iskender Gider was born in Istanbul, Turkey.
When he was nine years old, he moved with his
parents to Germany, where he went to school in
Cologne and Recklinghausen. Today he is a
commercial artist and an assistant professor at
the University of Essen. The things he most
likes to paint in picture books are elephants,
pigs, chickens, and foxes—especially sly foxes
like Rinaldo.